DESPERATION

John Tunnell

CONTENTS

In the twenty first century, in the land of America there lived a man whose name was Jacob. He was blameless and upright. He did right and shunned evil. He owned many businesses and was one of the richest men in the country at that time. The beautiful thing was that you would never know it by meeting the man. He was kind and humble. He was generous, but not only in front of the public's eye. He helped all that asked him and he had a true love of life and it shined through in the way that he treated people. Just being around the man was an inspiration. He seemed to glow. If you ever got the chance to meet him your day would be better and you would feel more confident.

It is easy to be intimidated by most rich people, but not Jacob. He had this peace about him that was unexplainable.

Jacob had a beautiful wife, but once again she wasn't just a trophy wife that so many aim for. She was a perfect woman. She was a great hostess. She was kind and a good mother. She was very understanding. She didn't nag. She supported Jacob in everything he did. She never had a bad thing to say about anyone. She truly had, not just a pretty face and a gorgeous body, but a beautiful soul.

Jacob had two wonderful children. A son named Taylor who was 6 years old and a daughter named Rose who was 8 years old. His children were the jewels in his crown. He loved his children like no man I have ever seen. They were always in his conversation and they were always in his heart.

Jacob was the greatest man among all the people of the West.

Chapter 1 - It Begins with a Dream

Jacob and his friend Frank are eating a business lunch in a nice restaurant. It is a celebration lunch to celebrate the fact that Jacob is about to make a huge business merger today that should double his net worth. The two have been friends for decades. Frank is Jacob's right hand man.

After they order their meal Frank congratulates Jacob. "Who would have thought that the greatest man in the world had room for improvement? I can't believe that the merger with Hope Technologies Hospitals is finally going to go through! You are going to be rich! Well richer! Maybe richest! Wow!"

Jacob kindly corrects his friend "I hope you don't think I am doing this for the money, Frank. The money is obviously going to be nice, but the truth is that the more you own the more it actually owns you. It is a responsibility. I am buying the hospitals because I want to do my part to make the world a better place. I think this is a great way to do it.

With the right attitude and the right funding we can fix almost anything. We must dream bigger and have faith. Anything you can imagine can be done. We have sent people to the moon. We can push a few buttons and talk to people on the other side of the world as if they are standing right next to us. We can access all the collective knowledge of the human race thanks to the Internet. Why is this? It is because someone had a vision. They dreamed it. They planned it. They found the time and the money to see it through.

I want to be that person. I don't want to just be remembered as a nice guy that was rich and generous. I want to make a difference, Frank. And I think these hospitals might be the way to do it. Perhaps we were put in this position for such a time as this? Maybe we are instruments in God's hand? Perhaps He is using us to bring about a drastic change for the good of all mankind? If we are short sighted and stubborn nothing will change."

Frank is used to the way Jacob speaks. It is as if everything he does has a mission and a meaning. But something seems different about this most recent transaction. It is as if Jacob has been quickened recently. Almost like he knows that his end is near and he wants to finish strong. It is like the sprint before the finish line. And still Frank is taken by surprise.

"You amaze me everyday, Jacob! How can you be dreaming of the future when the present is so great for you?" He gets distracted "Speaking of dreaming I had a weird dream last night. I dreamt that I was being chased all night long by something. I don't know what it was, but I was terrified. It felt dark and demonic. I felt like the devil himself was chasing me. It was difficult to breathe. My pulse was through the roof. I couldn't speak. I felt paralyzed. It was terrifying! Eventually I must have woken up. The strange thing was how real it felt while I was dreaming it. Then I woke up and I wondered how I ever believed that what I dreamt was true? My therapist calls them night terrors. Far worse and more real than your regular run of the mill nightmares. I have had them since I was a child. I have them less now, but wow! Intense!"

Jacob has been listening to Frank but is distracted by his phone. He lifts his eyes from a text message "I know what you mean. Last night I hardly slept a wink. All night I dreamt I was working on this project. It was so stressful because I couldn't really get anything done. I just kept trying and seemed to get nowhere. Then I woke up exhausted and nothing had been accomplished. I had done all that work and hadn't even gotten paid for it and then to top it off I had to go straight to work after I woke up and do the whole thing over. What a bummer, huh?"

Frank seems a little put out. "That's it! That's your bad dream! That's a walk in the park. I wish my subconscious were that tame. Do you have any real problems? Anyone in the world would gladly give everything they have to have your problems. I hope when you get these hospitals you have to spend some time in them, so that you can see the way other people suffer in this world. I mean, look, I know you had a tough childhood and I know that you worked with your own hands for everything you have, but have you forgotten what the common man has to deal with in the average day? You have become that rich guy that lives high up in an ivory tower far removed from any of society's problems. Did you even hear what I said?"

"I know it sounds bad. Maybe I should spend some time in my hospitals and soften my heart. You know, get to know the people again. I hope I don't come across wrong. I just want to be a good man. I just want to do what is right. When I have to give an account for my life I want to be proud of myself. That is all I ever wanted. Maybe I didn't fully hear you…"

While they are talking in the restaurant we are taken to another place. Jacob and Frank are still talking in the restaurant and they have been on a TV screen in a courtroom this whole time. It is in the background and none of the court is paying attention to the TV at this time. The courtroom is bright white. Everything in it is bright white. Every piece of furniture is white. The TV monitors are translucent and have data streaming across them constantly. It is as if the entire world is being judged from this courtroom. There are people all around making notes on their computers. There is a jury of faceless people. Everyone is dressed in white. The courtroom is very sterile. The judge never shows his face, even when he speaks.

Suddenly we notice a man kicking and screaming. He is begging for his life as he is being taken away in restraints. The prosecutor, Lucy, seems unmoved by his imminent demise. She is stoic and determined. She looks through her files smugly for the next case. An evil smile comes across her face, as she seems to actually take pleasure in ruining this poor soul. It is subtle. She tries to remain professional, but there is a sinister air to her character. Very matter-of-factly she says, "This world is filled with criminals. It is sickening. That is one less unrighteous villain walking the streets. The problem seems to be that they are all guilty. There isn't even sport in it any more for me. It's like shooting fish in a barrel. Everyone has a dark side they don't want anyone to see, but we all see it. Everyone has crimes that cry out to be punished. Everyone is guilty. Everyone has a closet filled with skeletons. Everyone has secrets.

I can win any case that comes my way. Bring on the next one. Pick anyone. I will try them and I will win, without effort and without breaking a sweat. Why do you even try to defend the guilty, Joseph? Don't you know they all have a special place waiting for them? And I will send them there."

Joseph is the defense attorney. He has kind eyes. He looks exhausted and beat down. You can see his heart sink with Lucy's words. It is as if he is fighting a battle that cannot be won. And yet he stands with resilience.

"What about Jacob?" he says "Look at the screen? That man is upright and there is no fault in him. He gives generously. He helps all that ask him. He doesn't abuse his power. He won't take a bribe. He is faithful. And there are more like him than you think. There are armies of people that quietly do right every day, regardless of any consequences to them. Try that man and he will come through shining. Mark my words."

Lucy looks at the screen in the courtroom for a moment. She recognizes Jacob and cringes a little. Her eyes are filled with hatred and rage. Her blood begins to boil. Her face turns red. She ponders for a moment as she takes a sip of water.

She composes herself and in a controlled tone says, "The man Jacob has a great reputation. You are right about that. But look at him. He has it all. Who wouldn't be upright in that situation? Take away all he has and he will curse the day he was born and that fake, holy facade will fade as quickly as the sun sets at night."

Joseph seems to immediately regret bringing up Jacob. "There is no need to do all that. I am just trying to remind you that even though we see lots of bad people, there are also many good ones that go unnoticed. Leave the man alone and let's get on to the next case."

Lucy smiles wickedly and continues to push the issue "You're afraid, aren't you? You're afraid that if he falls, which he will, that all this false hope you have in the human race will be shattered? Let's test the man! Let's watch him fall. How can you truly know what is in a man until he has been through the fire. Many talk a good talk, but does he have what it takes to go all the way? Let's see."

She turns to the judge "Your honor, I humbly ask that we have the opportunity to try this hypocrite, this Holy Roller, this wolf in sheep's clothing. I hereby accuse Jacob Mason and demand his trial begin immediately."

Joseph stands up quickly "Objection! This is ridiculous and unnecessary! Let the man go on in peace. He has done no wrong and nothing good can come of falsely accusing him."

Lucy snaps back "If he has done no wrong then he will stand through the trial and there is nothing to worry about. He is next. I demand my right as the prosecutor to try anyone I think may have need of punishment and whom I think is a threat to the public. It is the law!"

Although we cannot see the judge's face we can hear the reluctance in his voice. There is silence for a moment. Anticipation builds in the courtroom as the crowd awaits his reply.
He sighs. "Very well. Jacob may be tried. This is against my better judgment, but the letter of the law must be upheld. If we make exceptions for him than we must for everyone. We must uphold the laws we have sworn an oath to. You may take everything the man has Lucy, but you must not lay a hand on him. You cannot make him sick and you cannot kill him. Are we clear?"

Lucy is beaming with glee. She can hardly contain herself. "Yes, your honor. I'll get right on it."

Joseph is devastated. "I object, your honor. He has done nothing wrong."

The judge stands firm with his decision. "The prosecutor feels otherwise. If the man is as you say, then there is nothing to worry about."

Joseph seems desperate "But, your honor. He has done nothing..."

The judge cuts him off sharply "I have spoken. Go prepare to defend your man. He will need all the help he can get. Lucy is good at what she does, but I believe the man is ready. Go, do what it is that you do Joseph. Waste no time. You are the defender of the defenseless. As always, you may not reveal yourself for who you are or what you are doing. It is against our law and has consequences that are irreversible and severe."

Joseph bows his head "Yes, your honor. I will respect your judgment." He turns to leave the courtroom. Lucy has already hurried out eagerly. She seems to be wasting no time at all. As Joseph leaves the courtroom we notice the TV screen where Jacob and Frank are still eating their lunch. They have been completely unaware of the courtroom or any of the conversations about Jacob. Jacob does not realize that everything he has ever known is about to come crashing down. They continue in their conversation as if life will continue on as it always has, but that couldn't be farther from the truth.

Chapter 2 – All is Lost

Back at the restaurant Jacob and Frank are still eating lunch. The discussion has become heated. Frank's voice is raised "Ok Genius, if there is so much justice in this world than why do bad things happen to good people?"

Jacob calmly replies, "I don't claim to have all the answers. I just know there is a much bigger picture than I can see. What seems to be a tragedy while it is happening ends up being a blessing in the long run. Something happens in the storm that makes us better. I wish there wasn't pain. I wish there wasn't injustice, but we are in a fallen world and unfortunately sometimes the innocent have to pay for what the guilty have done. I know it doesn't seem right, but I have faith that there is always a good reason for everything we experience. Both the good and the bad have a purpose.

And if we are honest when we look back on the bad things that have happened in our lives these have actually paved the way for some of the best things that have happened in our lives."

Frank remains unimpressed "So where is the good reason when a child is molested? When a woman is raped? When an innocent man is murdered? When a war is waged against civilians instead of the armies that are meant to fight? Where is the justice in that? There are some things that are just wrong, no matter how you look at it. How do you make any of that stuff right? What if it happened to you? At what point will the price be repaid? At what point is justice satisfied?"

Jacob drops his head "Well, I hope it never does happen to me, Frank. But if it did I would like to think that I would have the grace I needed to stand under the pressure of it all. Furthermore, I would hope to find it in my heart to forgive whoever it was that wronged me. I am not a perfect person. If I don't want to be judged than I cannot judge someone else, even if they have wronged me. I don't have all the information. My reactions would be selfish. They would just be retaliation. They wouldn't be based on true justice.

Often hurting people hurt people. Generational curses are passed on from one victim to another until some strong person makes the decision to absorb the blow and not pass the pain on. I wouldn't want to continue to live as a victim over and over again. I would hope to have the strength to take my pain with a presence of mind that would allow me to see the other person's point of view."

Frank snaps back "That's easy to say now, but what if tragedy comes knocking at your door today and is relentless? What if you can't get away? Then will you want to forgive your persecutor? Won't you want revenge? Won't it make you furious? You simply don't know until it happens to you."

Jacob stands his ground "The only person you hurt when you hold a grudge is yourself. I wouldn't forgive them as much for their sake as I would for my own."

Frank continues "But why do bad things happen to people that don't deserve it? Where is the glory in that? What is the big plan? If God knows everything and He knows what we are going to do and what we are going to choose, if he knows us inside and out, then why does He allow the atrocities that we are forced to live with everyday?"

Jacob pauses for a moment to consider Frank's question "Let's say that God knew you were going to do terrible things in your life and so He just said no. He just spared everyone the hassle and put you straight into your final resting place... in hell. Would that be just?

Frank doesn't hesitate "Yes! Of course! If the innocent don't have to suffer, then yes!"

Jacob continues "Think about it from the other side. What if you never had a chance to make those decisions? What if someone else just told you one day that you would have done bad things and so now you are in hell being punished for what you would have done? Would that be right?"

Frank pauses "It does sound a little harsh, but still the end justifies the means."

Jacob smiles "On the contrary, the means determine the end. We have free will and so if we are to be punished we have to have the opportunity, the choice, to change and do the right thing.

What if God knew you would be a good man and so He just saved you the trouble and brought you straight to heaven. Would you know why you were there? Would you appreciate it? Would you even be the same person? There are certain rights of passage that we must pass through. The choices we make in life determine what we are and what we will be ...and what we deserve."

Frank mutters under his breath "How many people really get what they deserve, though? I mean really? There are bad people succeeding all over the place while good people suffer."

Jacob replies, "I think in the end everyone does. There is a judge that is just. He sees our heart and our motivations and there is no fooling him. Justice is there, if we will wait patiently for it."

Frank remains unmoved "I think that may be true sometimes, but sometimes we need to take justice into our own hands and set things right ourselves!"

Jacob is shocked "Wow, Frank. You're coming on a little strong today. Is there something you need to tell me? Is there something bothering you?"

Frank apologizes "Look, I'm sorry to be so harsh. I know we are supposed to be celebrating this merger. This should be a happy day. I'll shut up. It's just hard to hear about how everything bad happens for a reason from a guy that has it all. What bad stuff happens to you? You live a perfect life."

As Frank is saying this Jacob's cell phone rings. He looks down and looks back up at Frank. He tries to pay attention to Frank, but seems distracted. The phone keeps ringing. Jacob apologizes "Let me get this real quick Frank. It's my lawyer. Hopefully it is good news about the merger."

He answers the phone smiling "Ed, Talk to me. Tell me good things." Ed sounds somber "Jacob listen, all the papers are signed and we closed on the Hope Technologies Hospital merger early this morning."

Jacob seems eager "Great, I can't wait to get started on the changes we talked about. We are going to turn this thing upside-down!"

Ed tries to get to the point "Yeah, Jacob there's a problem, one of the accountants came and delivered a package to me an hour after we closed. It seems that the hospitals have racked up quite a debt."

Jacob is unmoved and remains eager "We already knew that though. What's the big deal? If they didn't have the debt, they wouldn't have sold so quickly and for such a low price."

Ed continues, "They have several lawsuits that are awaiting judgments to be paid. We need to talk in person. This is a lot more than we thought. This could break you. I'm sorry Jacob. Can you meet me at the office in an hour?"

Jacob looks like someone has kicked him in the chest. Like all the wind got sucked out of him. He tries to fake a smile. He takes a deep breath. "Yeah Ed, I'm on my way now. Don't stress, I'm sure this can be fixed. It is just money. I'll see you in an hour." Jacob hangs up the phone. He looks like distressed. His eyes drop. He looks down at the table.

Frank wants to know "What was that all about? It didn't sound good."

Jacob tries to brush it off "Oh, it was Ed. There was some glitch in the merger. I'm sure it's nothing. I've got to go." He motions to the waiter to bring the check. The waiter nods and walks toward the register. Jacob's cell phone rings again. He looks at the caller ID and smiles. He answers the phone "How is my beautiful wife today?"

In a very sweet voice his wife says "Sweetheart... you know how much I love you?"

Jacob rolls his eyes. "What do you need Laura?"

His wife sounds offended "Now, why do you assume I need something? I can be sweet. What if I just wanted to call and tell you how much I love you and how much you mean to me?"

Jacob laughs, "Cut to the chase Honey. I know that tone in your voice."

Laura acts put out "I can't believe you! I just called to say I love you. And to congratulate you on this amazing merger..."

She pauses. Jacob begins to apologize "Well, thank you. I'm sorry I was presumptuous…"

She continues "…And to see if you could pick up the kids from school? The nurse called and said they were sick."

Jacob exclaims, "I knew it!" As he is on the phone he pays the check and waves goodbye to Frank.

Laura doesn't give him a second to gloat "Listen, I know today is a big day for you, but I am getting my hair done and I just can't break away right now. I have stuff in my hair and it would just ruin it if I left now. And it is so expensive. I know how you hate to waste money."

Jacob seems mildly irritated "I wish I could, but I'm on my way to the office. Something came up and it's kind of an emergency."

Laura hears the concern in his voice "What is it Honey?"

Jacob brushes it off "It's not important. I'm sure it's just a mistake. Ed called and said that the financial sky was falling. I'll call Nancy and see if she can get a driver to go pick up the kids. I'll see you tonight. Have fun at your hair appointment. I'm sure you will look beautiful, as always. I love you."

She says in a high pitched tone "You're so sweet, Jacob. I love you too."

Jacob hangs up with Laura. He seems distracted and worried. As he is walking to his car he calls his secretary. He pulls out of the parking lot and onto the highway as the phone's answering system goes through a gauntlet of options to finally get to his own secretary.

As soon as she answers he says "Oh good Nancy, its Jacob."

Nancy's tone drops "Jacob, Have you seen the papers today?"

Jacob brushes it off "No, I've been busy. Why?" Jacob's car comes to a complete stop. There is bumper-to-bumper traffic as far as the eye can see. He looks around for an alternative route, but he is stuck. He slams his hands on the steering wheel.

Nancy continues, "You're on the cover!"

Jacob is irritated, "That's nice." Under his breath he mutters "Stupid traffic. Why don't they move these things off the road quicker? Some of us have places to be! How many things can go wrong in one day?"

Nancy ignores his complaints "So, about the paper... apparently, one of your employees at the maid service has been stealing from your customer's homes. They are calling you a ringleader. They say you are the head of some kind of a theft scam from your customers. The article says "Jacob Mason. His maids clean your house and then while they are at it, they clean out your house"

Jacob is furious, "That's ridiculous! Nothing could be farther from the truth"

Nancy braces herself, "I know, but they have frozen your businesses until litigation proceeds. I got served with the papers right before you called. Of course, you can't fire anyone or lay anyone off. Which means you, will still pay them, but you can't make any money. On top of all that you have to provide maid service from your competition's companies, Dust Bunnies and Maids and More, at your expense to all your customers until the whole thing is resolved."

Jacob is furious "That isn't right! I'll be bankrupt in a month and going to court could take years!"

Nancy is sympathetic "It's terrible. How are you going to make it through this? I know it took everything you had to get this merger done and now that is a flop too. You are finished Jacob!"

Jacob swallows a huge lump in his throat "Don't be silly! This is a simple mistake. No one is going to lose their job and I'm not finished, not by a long shot! This is just a bump in the road." He gathers himself "Listen, the reason I called was to see if you could get a driver to pick the kids up from school. Laura said they are sick. I love those little rascals, but I have a lot to deal with today."

Nancy smiles "I know. It's already been done. The school called me before they called Laura. They are on their way home right now. Our regular driver is sick too, but I got a fill-in."

Jacob seems relieved "Nancy, you are a lifesaver. I don't know what I'd do without you."

Nancy cringes "Don't say that, Jacob."

Jacob doesn't skip a beat "It's true. You're the best. You take care of everything for me. I would fall apart without you there at the wheel."

Nancy pauses and then quietly says "I am pregnant, Jacob. I wish I could have told you on better terms than this. You're going to be fine without me. I've been thinking about being a better mother and wife to my family anyway. I didn't know how to tell you, but I have wanted to quit for a while now. And now with this scandal and the new baby I know you will need the extra money, so I'm putting in my notice. I'll start cleaning out my desk tomorrow."

Jacob stops her "We'll talk when I get there. We'll all get through this. It's just a minor setback. The world doesn't just stop working all of the sudden. I'll be there shortly. See you soon."

About an hour later Jacob rushes into the office, obviously frustrated. Nancy is crying at her desk. Jacob doesn't even seem to notice.

He is talking before he opens the door "I'm sorry it took so long to get here. The traffic was terrible out there today! Goodness gracious! I mean I'm sorry these people got in a wreck, or whatever, but the rest of us have places to be. They should just get the mess out of the way." He ponders for a moment and then continues, "It was a pretty bad wreck though. I feel bad for the families. The axle broke off the back end of an eighteen-wheeler and rolled over a car. You couldn't even tell what the car was. They couldn't possibly have survived. It was flattened."

Nancy bursts into tears "What color was the car?"

Jacob seems mildly irritated "I don't know. Burned? It might have been green. It was hard to tell and I don't like to rubberneck. Traffic has to move on and there is nothing I can do to help them. I'm sure the proper authorities are taking care of the situation as sad as it may be. Look, that's not important. You look terrible. You don't have to leave. I'll give you a raise. Just please stay. Why are you crying?"

Nancy sniffles and takes a deep breath. She tries to compose herself. Her voice is cracking as she explains, "I got a call. The driver that picked up Rose and Taylor got in a car wreck. He had a green car, too. They wouldn't tell me the details, but they said it was bad and that you should get to the hospital right away. And ironically it is at the hospital that you now own. Jacob, I'm so sorry." She totally breaks down into tears and runs out of the room.

Jacob falls to his knees and begins to weep. He begins to think about the good times he has had with his children. He thinks about how much he loves them. He reflects on how casually he blew off picking them up today. He thinks of all the ways things could have been different. He plays through the scenario in his head. Perhaps if he had just made them a priority instead of worrying about his businesses all the time maybe this wouldn't have happened. He looks deeply disturbed. He lifts his head to heaven and shouts at the top of his lungs. "Why? What have I done to deserve this? A day shouldn't have this much pain! An entire life shouldn't have this much pain!"

Tears are streaming down his face. He is hyperventilating. The weight of this burden seems too much to bear. He bows his head humbly and composes himself. "...Nevertheless, I am not blameless. Naked I came into this world, and naked I shall leave. How can I accept the good things in life, and not the disappointments with them? I guess Frank is going to get his wish? I will feel pain today, and I will feel the bitter sting for all the rest of my days!"

He wipes away his tears and stands up slowly. He drives to the hospital. The world goes on around him but he hardly notices. He thinks about the last time he saw his children and how he didn't cherish the moment. He thought there would be a million more moments like this, but that would be the last time he saw them. All the petty things in life that don't matter had consumed all his time.

Images flash through his mind of his children in the car crash. He thinks about how terrifying it must have been for them. How horrific. How jarring. He is temporarily distracted by the thoughts of all of his businesses being brought to nothing in one day, but quickly comes back to his children. The truth is he is a great father. He loves his children. He looks out for them. He always has their best interest at heart. He teaches them life lessons. He is a great example. He listens. He is gentle with them. He has a tender heart. But in his mind he could have done so much better. He could have done more. It breaks his heart. He quietly weeps all the way to hospital.

When he finally arrives he runs inside as quickly as he can. The lady at the desk points him in the right direction. He walks into the room as if in a daze. His 8-year-old daughter Rose is hooked up to a breathing machine. She is unconscious. Her face is swollen and almost unrecognizable. She has a tube down her throat. She has wires and tubes all over her body. He walks up to her slowly. He is in shock. He whispers softly to her as he brushes her hair behind her ear. "I'm so sorry. I love you so much. I wish it was me laying here instead of you."

His wife walks in behind him with tears in her eyes. She shakes her head and starts to hit Jacob's chest repeatedly. "How could you let this happen? Our daughter is in coma! She may never wake up. And our son is dead! Why couldn't you just pick them up from school? Is your precious work that important that you let this happen to our children?" Jacob takes the hits. He is crying, but he isn't fighting back or trying to defend himself. Laura storms out of the room.

Jacob hangs his head. He drops to his knees. Tears are flowing uncontrollably. Quietly he says, "I'm sorry. Please have mercy on my daughter. Please. If not for my sake, than for hers. Please. I will give all I have to let her live. Please."

Chapter 3 – Some Skin in the Game

As we pull away from Jacob's crying and hear his plea we are brought back to the courtroom. Everything he has just experienced has been on display on the TV for everyone to see. Many in the crowd are wiping away tears from their eyes. Others have their mouths wide open. Lucy looks nervous, but keeps a cool emotionless expression. The judge clears his throat. The murmuring quickly ceases.

Joseph stands and faces the judge. He wipes a tear from his cheek. "There is no fault in him! Even though all he had is gone he still stands blameless. He has done no wrong. I implore you to end this now!"

Lucy snaps back viciously "Not so fast, Joseph. Not enough time has passed. He hasn't had time to let the pain sink in yet. It's the healing pain that hurts the worst. He is still in shock. Let the bitterness rot his soul a bit. Let him stew in his misery. I demand more time. It is the law."

With hesitation the judge replies, "Lucy is right."

Lucy needs to hammer it home so she continues, "Some men have been known to stand for a while, but strike his flesh and he will curse you, this court, and everything he has believed in. I will not stop until the whole man has been tested. There is no one perfect. He will fall. He will fall. You almost have to ask, is the rise even worth the fall, Jacob? Is it? You will be crushed. You will wish you had never been born."

Joseph interrupts, "Give the man back his life. Your honor, please! I implore you."

The judge shakes his head, "I believe Jacob to be a good man, but I cannot bend the law for him or any other man. He will be tested. Very well, Lucy, you may strike his flesh, but you may not kill him. This is a test, not murder. I have spoken." He bangs his gavel.

And as he does we are taken back to the hospital. Jacob is looking through the glass at his daughter in the hospital. She is on life support. She is unconscious and she is having a difficult time breathing. Jacob's wife is standing next to him. She seems cold and distant. Jacob is staring at his daughter. They are both sad. He starts scratching at a red bump on his arm.

Jacob is sorrowful "Oh, how I wish that were me instead of her. Poor Rose. Will she ever come out of this? Will she ever be the same again? I could handle this. I have had a good life. But she is so fragile and young. She is so innocent. I wish I had taken the time to pick them up from school. I wish I had been there. Why wasn't I there?

Laura turns and glares at Jacob "I don't know Jacob? Why weren't you there? Now our son is dead and our daughter is in a coma! Why didn't you protect her? That's what a father does!"

He is saddened "I don't know why. I'm sorry." With tears in his eyes, "I'm so sorry."

Laura is cold. She looks disgusted. She musters her courage and then unleashes on him, "I can't be with a man like you. I've known this has been over for a while, but I thought I would fake it through ...for the kids, you know."

Jacob is stunned. He looks confused. He tries to process what his wife has just said. "What are you saying?"

She quickly gets it out "I'm leaving you, Jacob!"

He panics, "Don't say that. We can make it through this…" He pauses and then asks seriously "Is there someone else?"

Laura is defensive, "No! I'm not like that. I just don't love you anymore. That's all. Especially after this. I can't even look at you the same. It's over!" She can't look him in the eyes.

He sees it in her reaction, "There is someone else isn't there?"

She is angry. "No!"

Jacob isn't buying it "What's his name? Do I know him? Who is sleeping with my wife?"

She breaks down under the pressure of his stare "It's Frank, OK! It's Frank! There I said it! I love Frank. You could never be half the man he is."

He starts to scratch multiple spots on his body. He looks down and they seem to be growing all over him. Almost like boils, dozens of them. "Frank, as in my best friend, Frank? Frank, like the Frank that has been working for me for the last ten years? Frank, like the Frank that I invite into my home and have over for dinner? That Frank? Who I break bread with."

Laura defends her lover, "Yes, that Frank. You are always at work. It's all you think about. All Frank thinks about is me. He treats me like I am special. I love him.

Don't get me wrong. I love you, too. But it's different. I love you like a friend, but I love Frank like a lover. He is passionate and exciting! But, ever since the accident I just can't look at you the same. I can't help but blame you for the whole thing."

Jacob is in shock. He can't believe what he is hearing. He is angry, but can't really react or think straight. He is itching more and the boils are growing and becoming more obvious.

"Why? How long? Where did you two... I don't feel good... I think I'm going to be sick... this can't be real..." he pinches himself "... am I dreaming this?"

Laura looks sinister. She almost resembles Lucy, the prosecutor. Not the way she looks as much as the way she is talking and her mannerisms. "Let go, Jacob. Just let it all go. Are you still holding on to your integrity? Just curse God and die!"

She looks at his arms that are now completely covered in large boils. They are oozing with pus. He has scratched a lot of skin off while he wasn't paying attention. He is bleeding through his clothes in several places. "Hey. What is that? What is happening to your skin?"

She calls out to the staff for help, "Someone come help my husband!"

Two nurses come around the corner. Laura is frantic "Look at him! What is that? How is this even possible?"

An older nurse tries to remain calm. She starts asking questions. She immediately reaches for latex gloves. Under her breath she says to the other nurse "I've never seen anything like this before. What do we do with him?"

The other nurse looks frightened. As she picks up a phone she says, "Stay calm. I'm sure the doctors will know what to do."

They look at each other as if to say there is no hope and no explanation. They put him on a stretcher and push him down the hall out of sight. Jacob is panicking and is breaking out more and more as they wheel him out. Laura is troubled and sits in a hospital chair. She puts her face in her hands and cries. Time passes. Frank walks in. He puts his arm around her and she kisses him.

Jacob is in another room. A nurse opens the door and he sees his wife kissing his best friend through the crack. A tear rolls down his cheek as the door closes. The nurse tells him this will help with the pain and then injects him with drugs. Jacob fades and quickly passes out. He looks horrible. It is a sad sight to see such a strong man reduced to nothing so quickly.

One week later Jacob is on top of the roof of the Hope Technologies Hospital that he owns and now is a patient of. It is late at night. He is in his hospital clothes. He is covered in sores and scabs. He has lost weight. Jacob is rambling to himself. He doesn't look well at all. The wind is blowing hard and a storm is coming. Very quietly, but slowly louder eerie thunder builds in the background. Jacob seems to be under a trance.

"I can't sleep. I can't eat. How can a person's life change so much in one week? I am covered in scabs and sores. They don't even have a name for what I've got. I can't take any medication because everything they have tried just makes it worse. I have never felt pain like this before. Not just in my body, but at the very core of my being. It's like my soul is on fire. Like I am being punished. Like I am burning away and there won't be much left of me soon. And yet, I am still here."

He remembers Laura smugly saying to him in his hospital bed: "Are you still holding onto your integrity? Just curse God and die!"

He continues to feel sorry for himself "Nancy is gone. I am on the verge of bankruptcy. My son is dead." A tear swells in his eye. "Rose is in a coma and there is little hope for her." His lip quivers and he starts to cry. "And for whatever reason Laura has decided to leave me in my darkest hour. I am alone and I am broken. And she is with another man, my best friend." He breaks into tears uncontrollably. Jacob imagines images of Frank and Laura together, intimately.

As he is saying all this we are taken to the courtroom again. Jacob is talking, but he is saying what Lucy is saying right after her.

Lucy is speaking as if she is Jacob. As she says something, he repeats it as if it were his own thought.

Lucy looks intently at the screen and whispers "It would be better for everyone if I just ended it all. It would be better for me. It is the only way to stop this pain, this torment of my very soul."

And then Jacob repeats what she just said word for word "It would be better for everyone if I just ended it all. It would be better for me. It is the only way to stop this pain, this torment of my very soul."

Lucy continues, "I'll just step off the building. There will be no more pain and I won't be missed anyway.

Jacob steps closer to the edge of the building. The storm comes closer, the wind picks up. It seems to be blowing him towards the edge. Tension builds as the wind picks up a little. Lightning crashes and thunder rolls.

"I'll just step off the building. There will be no more pain and I won't be missed anyway."

He begins to step off the building when he hears a voice from behind him. It is Joseph, the defense attorney, but he is dressed as a doctor. Jacob, of course, does not recognize him since they have never met. Joseph calls out to Jacob just before he steps off the building.

"I wouldn't do that if I were you! Don't you have a daughter in ICU? I think she will want to see her Daddy when she wakes up."

Jacob doesn't even turn around. He is downtrodden. "Don't you mean **if** she wakes up? It is hopeless! You can't understand the pain I am going through. The world would be a better place without me."

Joseph raises his voice "You've had a hard week, I know. I've been watching you, but all things happen for reason. Don't you want to know the reasons?"

Jacob turns around "You speak as if you know? We won't know the answers for a long, long time, if ever."

Jacob steps away from the edge of the building. The wind is stilled instantly. The storm is gone. He seems to be out of the trance he was in just a moment before. There is silence and a feeling of safety.

Joseph smiles, "I knew you wouldn't do it. We believe in you. Come with me. I want to show you something."

Joseph reaches his hand out to Jacob. They walk through the hospital to a high security area with a room full of beds. All the beds are full of people who are unconscious. They all seem to be on life support. At the far end of the room is a machine that resembles a virtual reality booth. It has a facemask, gloves, and other high tech accessories with wires sticking out of them. Jacob loves things like this and picks up the goggles and puts them to his face.

Joseph smiles and says, "Don't you think it is ironic that the day you buy this hospital is the day you end up needing it?"

Jacob puts the goggles down, "I don't think I need it. I don't know if it does any good. I feel like I've been brought here to die. I don't know if it is what I need, honestly. I don't have much hope left. So much for Hope Technologies, huh? I'm just early for my own funeral is all."

Joseph smiles calmly, "Lighten up. The darkest hour is just before dawn, Jacob. I am on your side. We will make it through. One of the major research projects we are working on at Hope Technologies Hospital is the Born Again project. We have been studying the power of the mind for many years. One of the amazing things about the human mind is its ability to fool itself. To believe a lie even when it becomes ridiculous to do so."

Jacob is unimpressed, "Speak English Doc."

Joseph continues, "You know how when you have just awoken from a dream it still seems a little real, it still haunts you, and when you start to think about it you wonder how you could have ever believed such crazy things?"

Jacob shrugs, "Yeah? Sure. So what?"

Joseph starts to get excited. He is passionate about his work. "Well, the major thing we have found about most people in comas is that they just need to wake up. After they have had time to heal their bodies, all that remains to do is let them wake up. We can't force them though. It's like leading a horse to water, but not being able to make it drink."

Jacob turns to Joseph intently. "You have my attention. So how does she wake up? What do we have to do?"

Joseph smiles apologetically, "Well, first she has to move past the denial that she is even in a coma at all. You see, in her mind, life is still going on as if nothing ever happened. She probably thought she came home from school last week and nothing changed. She doesn't think anything is wrong and she doesn't want to let go of a life that is just vanilla right now. For her, life never stopped. It goes on inside her mind. She doesn't think anything is wrong. The mind, the soul, whatever you want to call it just won't let go sometimes. In her mind she is probably doing homework or getting ready for bed or hugging your neck or playing on the swing set in your backyard."

Jacob is very confused, "But how do we get through to her? How do we bring her back?"

Joseph gets serious "It is a delicate process. If done wrong, she can refuse to believe the truth and bury herself deep in her own mind. She will run. Sometimes it will send the patient into shock. And in the worst-case scenario... they die. A comatose person must be gradually shown the truth and then finally make the decision on their own to wake up. No one else can do it for them, unfortunately."

Jacob is confused "So what does this machine do that can help? How do all the gadgets and money equal success?"

Joseph perks up, "Here is the miracle! We have found a way to get inside the head of the victim. To meet them where they are and talk them through the pain. We use this machine to communicate directly with their subconscious, right to their soul if you will. And, if we are lucky, we bring them to life again. They are in a way born again. I use the machine to go inside their head and talk to them. I walk the walk with them back to life. It's more than just a few words though. It truly is a journey and a test. Only the strong can do it, but your daughter is strong. Just like you are strong. I believe you are strong Jacob. Do you believe that?"

Jacob lowers his head, "I used to think so." His eyes start to water, but then swallows the pain. "What makes you qualified to do this?"

Joseph opens his shirt to show the scars on his body. He has deep scars all over him. "Because I was in a coma and I came out. I came back to life. And my father and I developed the Born Again program. We want to help people truly live. We want to help you Jacob. Will you let me help you? Jacob? Jacob?"

Chapter 4 - What are the Odds?

Jacob hears his name being called over and over. He is startled and wakes up in his hospital bed. Jacob looks disoriented, but wakes up to see an acquaintance named Bill hovering over him. Bill is shaking him, "Jacob... Jacob... wake up Jacob!"

Jacob rubs his eyes slowly. He looks confused. "Bill, what are you doing here?"

Bill puffs his chest a little in a self-righteous way and says overly sympathetically "I heard what happened. I came to talk with you, Jacob."

Jacob smiles "That was nice of you. You didn't have to do that. I just had the weirdest dream. It seemed so real. There was this really nice doctor who said he could help Rose out of the coma. He said they could see inside her head.

Bill is dismissive "Of course they can. It's called an MRI. And the results don't look promising. Jacob, I'll get to the point. What have you done to deserve this?"

Jacob is taken back by this "What do you mean Bill?"

Smugly Bill continues "I mean what sins have you committed that have made God so unhappy with you that your entire life has fallen apart? On the outside you seem holy, but there must be some hidden sin that merits this kind of punishment. Do you molest little boys?"

Jacob is shocked "No! What is the matter with you?"

Bill pushes more "Do you make snuff films?"

Jacob is disgusted "No!"

Bill is relentless "What do I need to know about you?" He stares into his eyes looking for some clue of immorality.

Jacob is very uncomfortable "What is the matter with you? Is this how you choose to comfort a man in pain? I haven't done any of these things. Don't be ridiculous!"

Bill points his finger at Jacob. His eyes are squinted. He is staring intently "There is something though. I will find out what it is. I have a priest friend who does exorcisms. I will call him and see if he can help. We need to purge you from your sins. I also know a prophet who can tell you your secrets. Maybe that will help?"

Jacob is irritated and offended "I just need some rest and I need my daughter to wake up."

Bill doesn't let up "Can't you see the connection? Bad things don't happen to good people! There must be some really bad thing you have done to deserve all this. What did you do to deserve this?"

Jacob is distressed "Nothing! Nothing! Sometimes things just happen! It's not my fault!"

Bill has a wicked look in his eyes "It's no fun is it? You have made your bed and now you have to sleep in it. I'm telling you, the chains that hold you down are the chains that you have made. There is no one to blame, but you. We must purge you! Just confess. Just let it out. What are your secrets? We all have them, what are yours?" He pulls out an old bible and starts waving it around.

The hospital door opens and a male nurse comes in to check on Jacob. The nurse looks irritated with Bill "I'm sorry sir, but you're going to have to leave. We need to perform some tests and you can't be in here for them."

Bill is furious "I don't have to leave! I have just as much of a right to be in here as you do! I know the rules!"

The nurse nods politely but sternly "You do have to leave if the patient asks you to. Would you like some privacy while we do these tests, sir?" He looks at Jacob. Jacob looks back at him as if to say thank you. He is relieved "I think that would be better, don't you? I could use some rest."

The nurse smiles gently at Jacob and then looks curtly at Bill "You heard the man. Please leave us." Bill leaves in a huff and slams the door. The nurse starts to work on tests and talks with him in the meantime. "Is that man a friend of yours?"

Jacob sighs "Oh, Bill? No, not really. I've known him for a long time, but he never has anything good to say. I know he goes to church and I think he means well, but he seems to be an accuser more than an encourager. I don't want to talk bad about him. I'm sure deep down he is a good guy. It just seems like he only comes during hard times in my life, and when he does... I only feel worse about myself after talking to him. Is that wrong to say about someone?"

The nurse proceeds checking diagnostics but talks as he does, "Just because someone says they go to church doesn't mean they have all the answers. The devil knows more about the Bible than any of us ever will. After all you will know them by their fruit. Do good and evil come from the same man? Does a river have salt water and fresh water? Does a tree grow apples and thorns?"

Jacob ponders, "Huh, I never thought about that?"

The nurse talks as he works "A man had two sons and he told them both to go out to work the field that day. The first son said he would, but later did nothing. The second son refused to do any work, but later felt guilty and did all the work he was assigned. Which one of these did what his father asked?"

Jacob looks at him, "The second son I suppose."

The nurse smiles at him "Things aren't always what they appear to be. Sometimes the one screaming the loudest about how holy they are is the one that is the farthest away from being holy. And sometimes the man that quietly encourages you as your friend is the very one that God has sent to help you. Compassion is rarely loud."

He looks up at the nurse "What is your name, anyway?"

The nurse replies, "My name is Michael, but that's not important. OK, we are all done for today. Get some rest. We'll get this thing fixed before too long. I can tell you will make it through."

Jacob has desperation in his eyes, "How can you tell, Michael? How do you know I will make it?"

Michael smiles, "Because you have the right people on your side ...and you are a good man. We believe in you, Jacob."

Jacob looks puzzled "How did you know my name?"

Michael pauses a little nervously, but then points and says, "It's on your chart. I always want to know my patient's names. You...guys give my life a purpose."

Jacob's pain seems to melt away for a moment, "You know, in that light you look like an angel."

Michael turns around to close the door, "Get some rest." Jacob closes his eyes. Michael closes the door. He drifts off to sleep.

Later that night Jacob is hungry so he walks down to the cafeteria and starts to eat. He sits next to another patient, who is covered in tattoos and piercings and looks very rough. Jacob asks the man, "Do you mind if I sit here?"

The man is short with him. "Whatever! I don't know why you want to eat this slop. It makes my stomach turn, just like this whole world we live in. What's your story, anyway? You look terrible!"

"My name is Jacob Mason." The man grunts "Snake". There is an awkward silence. Jacob doesn't want to seem rude. "Snake? Is that your name?" The man looks irritated, "Right! Do we have a problem?" Jacob gets defensive "No, it's just a little unusual. Did your parents name you that?"

It seems obvious that Snake doesn't have much social grace, "It's on my birth certificate. Do you want to start something?"

Jacob trying to be diplomatic, "No, I'm sorry. I'd shake your hand, but they don't know if what I have is contagious."

Snake shakes his head, "That's cool. I don't want to be your friend anyway. You look too rich for my blood. I come from the other side of the tracks, if you know what I mean. Wait. Did you say Jacob Mason?"

Jacob almost forgot his status, "Yes"

Snake laughs in his face, "Don't you own this hospital? I read about you in the papers. Didn't your wife cheat on you? Didn't your son die? And your daughter is in a coma? Didn't you go bankrupt? Ha! Ha! Ha!"

Jacob is offended, "What's funny about that?"

Snake is laughing uncontrollably, "Man, it must suck to be you! I mean I thought I had it bad. So was the rise really worth the fall?" He starts coughing.

Jacob's countenance falls, "I'm sure I'll bounce back. It can't last forever, right?"

Snake clears his throat and looks around suspiciously. He gets really serious, "Yeah, whatever. Man, if I were you I'd kill that tramp of a wife of yours for doing that to you. Kicking a man while he's down, that's just not right. Has she even come to see you?"

Jacob defends his wife, "No. She doesn't want to get what I've got." As the words are coming out of his mouth he realizes how bad that sounds.

Snake rolls his eyes, "She just doesn't want to feel guilty for being a dirty cheater. Between you and me, I know a guy that will take care of her." Snake runs his finger across his throat from ear to ear. "Cheap, too. Not that that matters to a guy like you. Money is just pieces of paper to people like you. You probably wipe your butt with hundred dollar bills, don't you?"

Jacob is shocked, "No. That is my wife you are talking about you know."

Snake grabs Jacob's hand and starts writing a number on his arm. "Here is the guy's number? You just say the word and it's done, man. I bet he'd do it for free just because it's you. It's good to have friends in high places."

Jacob pulls his hand back before Snake can write the whole number on his arm, "I'm not that kind of guy."

Snake winks at him and nods "You don't have to be. I'm trying to do you a favor, man. You just say the word. No one will know. It'll be our secret and as you can see I'll be dead soon. I have stage four-pancreatic cancer. Our secret will go to the grave with me...and of course… her. Ha! Ha! Ha!" He starts coughing a hoarse grisly cough.

Jacob is deeply offended "No thank you. Stay away from my wife. Stay away from me. I am a peace-loving man even if I have had a bad run of luck lately."

Snake laughs, "Run of bad luck! That's an understatement if I ever heard one! Your name should be Job, like the guy in the Bible who lost everything. What else could possibly go wrong in your life?"

Jacob is disheartened, "I'm not really hungry. Have a good night, Snake." As he is walking away he turns around. "Stay away from my wife." Jacob walks away and leaves his food at the table.

Snake calls after him, "You just say the word Jacob. I'll make it happen for you. Vengeance is the only cure for a broken heart."

As Jacob walks into the hall he mumbles to himself, "If he only knew how tempting that was. How could she do that to me? I hate her for this! I know I shouldn't, but I do. I hate her!" Anger swells inside of him. A tear rolls out of his eye. "How could she leave me? I am so alone. In all my pain there is no one here to comfort me. I hate her for doing this to me!"

He cries for a moment and then collects his thoughts, "I'm sorry. What is the matter with me? It's like a battle is raging within me. I'd love for that part of me to die. I wish the evil coward in me were gone and that the strong, righteous me ruled. I just want my life to be good again. I want some peace. I need a break from all this torture."

As he is talking to himself he walks by a lounge area. A television set is on in an otherwise empty room. He walks by and then stops. He turns around and sits on the couch. "Maybe some TV would get my mind off of me for a while. I just need to relax my troubled spirit." He picks up the remote control and starts flipping through the channels

"Sports, huh? Nope. Wrestling, what a joke? It's not fake, whatever. Nope. Nope. Nope. Today's music is horrible. Nope. A TV evangelist, huh? That should be a good laugh." He puts down the remote and settles in.

From the TV the evangelist is speaking in a very personal tone, "Don't you feel like God is trying to tell you something? I know that everyone of you watching this show right now is dealing with things that are difficult. Many of you have had tragedy. Many have had loss. Many of you have been cheated and cheated on. It isn't right. You want to hurt someone. You want revenge."

Jacob sits up a little, "What are the odds of that?"

The evangelist continues, "Forgiveness is the only way to free yourself from the pain. You see nothing you do is a secret. Everything you do is on display, even the dark things, even the private stuff. And God speaks to us each in his own language. Not just English or French or German or Spanish. He knows us intimately. Each of us has his own journey. The same principals apply to all of us, but the road we take is unique and deeply personal.

You are never alone. He is always there when you need Him. He knows your every thought. Remember that. You call on Him and He will be there. Whenever temptation comes there is always a way of escape that He provides. If you believe and stay strong, you will never fall! Hallelujah! You will make it through. It's a hard road, but you will make it. We believe in you. We believe in you. You're going to make it. You're going to make it, Jacob Mason!"

Jacob's jaw drops open, "What! How did he know my name?" He looks around the room frantically. No one is there. He is alone. He doesn't see any cameras in the room. He puts his head in his hands and closes his eyes.

Chapter 5 - He Who Seeks, Finds

Jacob wakes up in his bed and he is alone. He is confused. Holding his head and rubbing his eyes he sits up and speaks to an empty room, "I'm so confused. I don't know what is real anymore. This is starting to scare me. If I could just plead my case with the watcher of men. If I could just speak to someone face to face about my life and what is happening." He speaks as if he can be heard.

"A few weeks ago I knew what was real and my life was good. Now, I can't seem to keep it together. It's all a blur. I want to know the truth. What is happening to me? Please, hear me! Please hear me, oh watcher of men. Please let me bring my case before you. What have I done to deserve this? If I have committed some crime or some sin let me know. I will make it right. I'm sorry. Just please give me peace. Please, please, please...."

We are brought back to the courtroom. The people are watching Jacob's every move. The court looks shocked that he is actually addressing them. They are looking at each other in confusion.

Joseph doesn't skip a beat, "Your honor, you heard him. Permission to speak to Jacob. Permission for him to speak to us. Permission for a mediator. Your honor, he is ready. He asked for it. I implore you."

Lucy stands up quickly "Objection! He's just rambling. He doesn't know what he is saying. He is just thinking of vengeance and his mind is drifting. Give him another few seconds and he will ask for you to kill his wife and that scumbag, Frank."

The judge perks up. There is hope in his voice. "Over ruled. He asked and he shall receive. Joseph, I grant you a mediator. Lucy, you will stay silent while they talk. No interruptions. You'll get your turn. Do you understand?"

Lucy looks defeated, "Yes, your honor." Her eyes are angry and downcast like a scolded child.

The judge addresses Joseph, "Send Eli. He's a good man for the job."

Back in the hospital a man named Eli walks into Jacob's room, "I heard you from outside the door, Jacob. Am I interrupting?"

Jacob looks embarrassed, "Eli, what a pleasant surprise. No you're not interrupting. I'm just feeling sorry for myself. Life isn't always what you think it should be, is it?" He wipes tears from his face.

Eli grabs a box of tissues and offers them to Jacob. Compassionately he says, "No, I wish it were. Life is a complicated mess sometimes. Talk to me Jacob. What's on your heart?"

Jacob takes a deep breath and sighs, "I'm just confused, that's all. I feel like a real head case right now. I don't know if it's the illness or Laura leaving me or what, but I've got to tell you I'm a mess. I just want some answers."

Eli looks at Jacob mercifully, "Answers to what exactly?"

Jacob becomes self-conscious of how crazy he is about to sound, "You'd laugh if I told you. I don't think anyone would understand."

Eli gently says, "I'm curious. I won't laugh and I won't criticize. Tell me what answers you seek."

Jacob chuckles, "Well, OK, but you asked for it. I want the truth. I want to know what is wrong with me. I want to know why total strangers know intimate details about me. The guy on TV called me out by name! I want to know why all this happened. I want to know why I feel like everything I am doing recently has just been a string of dreams. I feel like I'm going crazy. I feel like I wake from a dream only to enter another stranger dream! I want the answers that I deserve."

Eli smiles eagerly, "Are you really ready for those answers though?"

Jacob is mildly irritated, "Of course, I'm ready. I wouldn't ask if I wasn't ready."

Eli gets serious, "What would you be willing to lose to get these answers you seek?"

Jacob laughs to himself, "I don't have much else to lose. Everything I have is gone anyway."

Eli shakes his head and smiles. "Not everything. Not yet."

Jacob looks concerned, "Ok, be more specific. What's it going to cost me for the answers, and how do you know them anyway?"

Eli continues, "That depends. Do you want the answers that you want to hear? Or do you want the truth?"

Jacob looks confused, "The truth, of course."

Eli looks at Jacob, "The truth, the real truth will cost you... your reality."

Jacob is very confused, "What's that supposed to mean?"

Eli is cautious, "If you knew the whole truth about yourself, you would have to let go of everything you believe and trust me to help you through to the other side. Do you want the whole truth, or are you comfortable where you are now?"

Jacob pauses to seriously think about the question. He considers what he believes the options are and then answers, "I want the whole truth. I will give all I have to know the answers. I am tired of the lies."

Back in the court everyone is hushed in awe as they listen intently. Joseph speaks and then Eli repeats him back in the hospital. Joseph has been speaking through Eli this whole time.

Joseph says, "Very well, then. Come with me." On the monitor we see Eli say the same thing at the same time, "Very well, then. Come with me." They begin to walk out of the hospital room.

Joseph pauses and looks at the judge, "With your permission, your honor."

The judge seems to know what he is talking about, "Granted."

Eli walks Jacob down the hall to his daughter's room as they talk, "First let's go see how your daughter is doing. Do you remember when we talked about the Born Again project where your daughter could be born again into life with the rest of us?"

Jacob stops walking. He is very confused "I never talked about that with you... did I?"

Eli is gentle, "Don't you remember? You thought that was a dream, but that was me. I know this is hard, but you asked for the truth."

Jacob looks around the hall. No one seems to be in the hospital, but them. All the normal busyness has ceased completely. There is an eerie silence. "You're kind of freaking me out. How did you know about that?"

Eli continues walking and Jacob follows him into his daughter's hospital room. Jacob gets emotional, "Look at how calm she is. How I wish that were me instead of her in that bed."

Eli cringes, "Funny you should say that."

Suddenly a voice comes from above in Rose's room over the PA. It is the judge's voice from the courtroom. His voice is deep and ominous. He speaks with authority and conviction, "It is time. Show the man the truth! Jacob Mason you are about to have the answers that you seek."

All of the sudden Jacob falls to the ground and his spirit rushes, seemingly, to somewhere else in a hospital bed that is strange to him. He watches his body fade and then everything goes black. His eyes open abruptly to see his son, daughter, wife, and friends (including Frank) standing over his bed. They all start screaming and panicking. They act excited and call for the doctor. "He opened his eyes" Laura says.

You can tell it is the same people, but they look different. They are dressed different and are all dressed in white. Jacob looks at his arms and there are no boils. Jacob screams in horror. His spirit rushes away from that place and back to the floor in the room with Eli. He looks at himself in a hospital bed. His daughter is gone. He lays on the floor for a moment stunned. Eli reaches down and puts his arm around Jacob.

Eli tries to comfort him, "I'm so sorry, Jacob. Your daughter is not in a coma."

Jacob is still in shock, "I know." He says.

Eli hesitates, "You are."

Jacob struggles with the reality of it, "I know. But. That's impossible! I know who I am." He paces the room frantically, "I can walk and talk." He grabs a table, "I can feel stuff. I can move." He carefully makes sure that his hand won't go through Eli. "I can talk to you. How could that be true? It can't be true! I'm not in a coma."

Eli is calm and methodical, "Do you remember when we talked about the denial a coma patient goes through? The first step is realizing it is true. Now we just have to wake you up. More specifically YOU have to wake you up. But I am here to help. There is one way out. There is one door inside your mind that must be opened to wake you up and only you can open it. Are you ready to walk with me?"

For some reason Jacob resists, "I need some time to think about all this. I am confused. I still don't know if what you are saying is true. Leave me alone for a while." He points to the door and gestures for Eli to leave.

Eli is cautious, "I understand. It's always hard at first. The best thing to do is come out while it's still fresh for you. Will you follow me?"

Jacob is in a stupor. He looks like the rug was just pulled out from under him and he is trying to figure out what just happened, "Give me some time. Just give me some time. I need to think."

Eli presses a little harder, "Every time you say yes, it is easier and easier to say yes, but every time you say no, it is easier and easier to say no. Every time you make a choice there is a consequence. You have a family out there who loves you. Come with me and we'll go to them. What do you have to lose? Don't wait. It just gets more difficult if you do."

Jacob looks like he just saw a ghost. He is in a daze, "I just need some time to think. This is a lot to take in. Please leave me, now."

Back in the courtroom Lucy shouts loudly "You must do what he says. Leave him now. It is my turn! I need a mediator too. I want a tramp. Give me Crystal."

Joseph looks defeated. The judge yields, "Very well. Send Crystal."

Jacob is rocking back and forth on the floor in confusion. Lucy sends a beautiful woman to tempt Jacob. Crystal starts running her fingers through Jacob's hair, "It's not so bad you know. There is a lot of power in here if you know how to use it. If you have believed all this so far, then that means anything your mind can imagine can be done for you. Imagine the possibilities! Imagine the desires you could fulfill."

Jacob doesn't even question the fact that this girl has just appeared and knows what is going on, "I guess you're right, huh?"

Crystal grabs his hand, "Don't guess, touch. Touch me. Let's celebrate a new life together inside your mind. I know you want to. Touch me now."

Jacob pulls back, "You are beautiful... and sexy... and oh, hot... but I shouldn't...I am married!"

Crystal dismisses his argument, "Are you really? How much of what you believe to be true is actually true anyway? Where was the splice in your life? Do you really have a wife at all? How long have you been trapped in here?" She looks around.

Jacob is confused as he ponders her questions, "I ...I... don't really know."

Crystal seems confident, "I do. It's a lot longer than you think." She gets close to him and whispers in his ear, "Take me now. Don't think about it, just do it! I'm so hot for you right now, Jacob."

Jacob is tempted but he tries to push her away, "I just keep thinking how bad it hurt to know that Laura had cheated on me. Even if it isn't real, I just can't. Look, you are gorgeous, really you are, but I think you should leave."

Jacob closes his eyes for a moment and he is instantly on top of the roof with Crystal. She starts to hover and lifts her hands menacingly, "Anything you can imagine! Jump from the building! You won't die! It's not real! Watch!"

Crystal jumps, but doesn't fall. She just hovers above the ground and then flies back to Jacob. "None of this is real. It feels real. It looks real. But it isn't. You can't hurt yourself in here. Not really anyway."

She flies back to the edge of the building again. She looks over eagerly. She jumps off and then flies right back to him, "And now it's your turn. Jump! Free yourself! Free your mind from the chains that enslave you now. The chains that hold you down are the chains that you have made. Jump and be free with me! We can rule this world together."

Jacob walks over to the edge and then hesitates, "How do I know I won't fall?"

Crystal looks like she wants to push him, but she can't physically do it. She is frustrated, "Have some faith… in me, Jacob. Would I do anything to hurt you?" She smiles a sinister smile.

Jacob is very cautious, "I just met you. I don't know yet, but that doesn't look safe to me. I don't feel like you area a good person with my best interest at heart. You already asked me to cheat on my wife."

Crystal scoffs, "How would she ever know anyway? This is in your head. It's a dream. It's not real. She can't fault you for that, can she?"

Jacob stands firm, "I don't want to do wrong, even if it is fake. Wrong is wrong, plain and simple."

He closes his eyes for a moment and he is taken to the top of a mountain. The wind is blowing hard and a storm is coming. Lucy is there and she is tempting Jacob with tremendous fervor.

"Look Jacob, let's reason together shall we? I used to be a helper like Joseph... Eli... whatever. I helped him start the Born Again project. I would take what seemed like forever trying to help someone out of a coma. Most of the time they never come out anyway. Then every once in a while someone actually comes to grips with the fact that they are comatose. Let's say they actually make it out. Then they go back to the same disgustingly pathetic life they had before. After a while, and kind of by accident, I learned what you could actually do in here. Anything! Anything is possible inside the human mind! Anything! Watch this!"

With the wave of her hand a feast is laid before them. Then naked women appear, lots of them.

"You want something? Bang! There it is! Just like that! Anything! Why would I leave? Come join me, Jacob. Those that do join me have a much happier existence in here. I control this world. I can make it easy or hard for you. Do you want the boils gone? It is done for you."

She snaps her fingers and the boils disappear.

"Do you want vengeance? It is done for you?" He sees Frank and Laura together in bed and then they are murdered. "Do you want your life back? Do you want your money? Security? Your perception of reality? Anything you ask will be yours. Just bow before me. Let's work together. It can be lonely in here and I need a good man. And you, Jacob, are a good man. I want you to be mine. Kiss me. Join me. Bow to me. Say you are mine!"

Jacob hangs his head, "You have succeeded…" Lucy starts wringing her hands eagerly. "in thoroughly freaking me out beyond anything I thought possible. If they had an award for that sort of thing, you would win it. Trust me. I don't even know what to say. Wow!"

Lucy's mood changes, "I can also make this existence of yours horrific. I can make it worse than you could ever imagine. Your mind is my playground and those who aren't with me are against me. I will gladly make your life a living hell."

She shows him gruesome things. Blood, pain, destruction, famine, loneliness, war, stench, and horror.

"But, I don't want to have to resort to that with you. I…" She pauses. She gulps and continues, "…love you. I want to help you enjoy this place. Just say the word and anything you ask for is yours. You could rule the whole earth, the whole universe. Anything you can imagine. Will you bow to me?"

Jacob pauses and thinks about the consequences both ways.

"I thought about it and I would rather accept the consequences then bow to you. You don't seem like a very nice person and I don't want anything to do with you or anything you represent. I'm sorry I called you beautiful. Beauty is more than skin deep. Beauty comes from the inside, from your soul. And from what I have seen your soul is ugly. I want you to leave now, please."

Lucy is furious, "You fool! Do you know what I can do to you?"

The judge's voice comes from the sky, "You must leave. He asked you. He is in control. Leave the man alone."

Lucy's spell starts to break. She fades away in a frenzy, but as she does she screams, "You haven't seen the last of me, Jacob Mason. When you wake up you will have the boils again and your life will be as it was before you met me. You should choose more wisely. I can make you powerful or destroy you!"

The judge is stern, "Lucy, Now!"

Chapter 6 - Why Are You Running?

Jacob wakes up in the hospital bed again covered in sweat and in a panic. His heart is racing. He is once again covered in boils and is in pain. He looks around the room frantically, but he is alone.

"If I had only known what pain awaited me I would have wished to never be born. I will never smile again. I will never laugh again. All the people that I held dear have abandoned me. I am alone...forever. Is there no escape from this hell? Is there no way out? Is there life after death? Is THIS life after death?

Did I do something horrible to deserve this, and this is my punishment? How long have I been here? I wonder if any of what I consider to be life is real at all? Am I going crazy? What is the matter with me? I don't even know what's real any more! Someone please save me from myself! What have I done to deserve this? What have I done wrong, so that I can make it right? Why have I been singled out?"

The door opens and Bill walks in. He leaves the door open when he walks through.

"You have been singled out because you are a bad man, Jacob! Why else would all this happen to you? Look at you. It's disgusting. Grovelling here all alone. You have oppressed all the little people in your life, and now that your life is over you get to feel the sting of their pain. You should have been a better man, Jacob. What are you not telling me?"

Jacob can hardly believe it, "Why do you choose to kick a man while he is down? Is there no mercy in your heart? If I saw you in this mess I would try to offer words of encouragement, not accusation. I have done no wrong to deserve this. If I could just speak face to face with my accuser I would be able to defend myself, but I guess that isn't a privilege that I am granted."

Bill ignores everything Jacob just said, "Why did your wife cheat on you? Because you worked too much! You neglected your own family! You worshipped the almighty dollar!"

Jacob defends himself, "That's not true. I did what I had to do. I was a good husband and a good father."

Bill scoffs, "A good father! Ha! Would a good father let some stranger take his children home to die or be crippled? Wouldn't a good father protect his children? I think so! But your son is dead because of you! And your daughter is in a coma. There is nothing good about you, is there Jacob?"

Jacob is defeated, "That wasn't my fault. It was an accident. Give me some comfort. Stop with the pain."

Bill is relentless, "Comfort I can do, but I think you know what it will cost you?"

Jacob is confused, "What are you talking about Bill?"

Bill looks intently at Jacob, "I believe there is an offer on the table from a lovely lady who wants to help." He gestures his arm towards the door. All of the sudden Lucy walks in. She is in her true form, the one from the courtroom.

Lucy smiles and tilts her head, "So Jacob, how long must this go on? Are you ready for relief? Are you ready to be the master of your universe? Bow to me!"

Jacob is exhausted, "I...I....I wish I could, but it just doesn't seem right. Please leave." He sounds pathetic and defeated.

Snake walks in and says, "I could kill that cheating wife of yours. I could take care of all your enemies. I know all the right people. You could live an easy life like before, better than before."

Jacob is desperate, "Stop. Please stop."

Frank walks in and says, "Laura loves me, not you. Are you just going to lie there? Get up and fight me. Take your revenge. I was your best friend and I betrayed your trust. I slept with your wife.... again... and again...and again. She called out my name instead of yours. I was in your bed with her. I lied to your face. I stole your money. I was the one responsible for the theft ring at the maid service. I have set your perfect life ablaze. And I have loved every minute of it. I did it on purpose to intentionally hurt you. I have always hated you. You think you are so perfect. You have a perfect life. Welcome to your nightmare. But it isn't your fault. It's mine!"
Jacob is in tears. He can't believe what he is hearing. He is shaking uncontrollably. His face is red with anger. He is grinding his teeth.

Snake gets in his face and yells, "I can kill him if you give the word. I know you want me to. I see it in your eyes. Say it and it's done! He deserves it. Did you hear what he did to you? No one will blame you. Let me kill him now."

Frank taunts Jacob, "God knows I deserve it! Do it Jacob. Kill me. Or have him do it. I don't care. Kill your best friend. Kill your betrayer. Kill your Judas."

Jacob is torn, "Why do you torment me? I just want it to be the way it was before. I just want my life back. I just want my sanity back. I am totally losing it."

Lucy comforts him, "I know Sweetie, that's all we want for you. Just say the word and it will be done for you. We are here for you." She puts her arm around him.

Jacob ducks away from Lucy, "You are not good! I want you to leave now. If you really must do what I say, then I demand that you leave me alone!

Jacob drops to his knees. The room clears immediately. All the people just get sucked right out the door and seem to disappear. Then the room itself disappears. Jacob is in the middle of a field. All is quiet. It is eerie and still. The wind blows gently. He hears something rustle in the brush. He looks around and sees that it is a lion. It pounces out to attack. Jacob starts to run. He runs for a long time. He seems to be in slow motion. His legs won't work like they should. The lion is tireless. Jacob runs and runs and finally realizes his fate.

He is exhausted and out of breath. He turns to face the lion that is now rushing at him. The lion pounces as if it is coming in for the kill. Jacob loses all hope and sighs. His shoulders slump. He braces himself for death. The lion stops and stares in his face. The lion breathes heavily on Jacob. He opens his mouth and roars loudly. Jacob is shaking with fear. Then he speaks to Jacob. "Why are you running from me?"

Jacob is terrified. He is panting. He is out of breath. He screams back, "Because you want to kill me?"

The lion is still breathing heavily, "That is very presumptuous of you. Do you know who I am?"

Jacob is still terrified but also confused by the question, "A lion... I don't know?"

The lion looks intently into Jacob's eyes, "I am your courage. Why are you running from your courage? Turn and face your fears, Jacob. Stop being afraid. Be brave. Be the man you were meant to be."

Jacob dismisses the lion's words, "So you aren't going to eat me?"

The lion brushes over Jacob's question, "Things aren't always what they appear to be. Don't you think it's time to move on?"

Jacob is frustrated, "Move on to what? I think I might be losing it! I'm talking to a freaking lion for Heaven's sake."

The lion continues, "I saw you in the hospital room. I saw you open your eyes. I know you know the truth. You know that your wife didn't really cheat on you. You know your children aren't really hurt. You know that none of this is real. Yet you still hold a grudge. Why does this upset you? Are you going to be owned by something that isn't even real?

Forgiveness is a funny thing you know. When you forgive someone it's like setting a captive free... and later you find that the captive was you. Wake up Jacob. Leave this behind you. What are you holding on to?"

Jacob has a puzzled look almost of relief, "I see what you mean, but I am confused. All I ever wanted to do was make the world a better place."

The lion replies, "Don't ask yourself what the world needs. Ask yourself what makes you come alive, and do that, because what the world needs is people who have come alive. Wake up Jacob. There are keys to life. You must find them and walk through the door. Come join us. I am your courage, Jacob. I am in you.

This last statement irritates Jacob, "You are all in me! You are all just in my imagination! I just want some peace and some time to think."

The lion shakes his mane, "You have two choices. The first is a hard narrow road, but in the end it is rewarding and you will have life. The second seems easy and has temporary advantages, but is hollow and empty and miserable and in the end costs you your life and eventually your soul. The choice is yours. Choose wisely."

Jacob squeezes his eyes shut several times. He shakes. He clenches his fists. "I have tried to wake up. I have tried to find the clues, but I don't know where they are. I am lost! Give me a clue. Please help me!"

The lion exhales loudly, "Do you think that just because you said a few words it will all be over? That only gets you started! That is only the beginning. You must follow through... or it is worthless. There is a journey set before you. Choose wisely. Follow through to the end and you will do fine."

Jacob falls to his knees and closes his eyes. He opens his eyes to talk to the lion, but he is back in the hospital room. Eli is in the room. Jacob is confused, but almost seems to expect the weirdness at this point.

Eli is standing over him in the hospital room, "Where can the answers be found? Where does wisdom dwell? It is not in the land of the living. You have come to this place for a reason, Jacob. What is that reason?"

Jacob doesn't even lift his head, "I don't know. I'm so confused."

Eli asks Jacob rhetorically, "Do you know how they find gold these days?"

Jacob doesn't see the point, "Look for nuggets in the river, I don't know?"

Eli smiles, "Back in the old prospector days maybe. These days it is lot harder to come by. First you have to look for signs that show where gold might be. For this they send in teams of geologists to work for years. They map out where the gold could be. This costs millions of dollars. Then when they finally do have a clue they start to blast out rock. They have to dig miles beneath the surface to where no man has been before.

Then they blast the rock out of its comfort zone and bring it to the surface. But that's not the end. After that they have to refine it. In the old days, they used to purge the rock with fire until they were finally left with pure gold."

Jacob seems intrigued, "Now how do they do it?"

Eli continues, "They pulverize the rock into powder and then add chemicals to it in huge vats. First they filter out all the metals from the rock. Then step-by-step they take away everything else until all that is left is pure gold."

Jacob shrugs, "That seems like a lot of hassle."

Eli keeps talking, "In a good gold mine these days you would be lucky to get a tenth of an ounce of gold out of a ton of rock. And that's in a good one. It costs about 80 million dollars just to set up a mine."

Jacob does some math in his head, "It hardly seems worth it?"

Eli brightens up a bit, "With crews working around the clock all week that same mine makes two eighty-pound gold bricks a week."

Jacob remains unimpressed, "Why even bother? That's such a lot of work and money for such a small return on your investment."

Eli concludes, "Because that is several million dollars a week!"

Jacob is shocked, "That's some cash! I could handle that. It sure is a lot of work though."

Eli points at Jacob, "You have treasure in you that is much more precious than gold. You have to believe that."

Jacob drops his head, "You might have the wrong guy."

Eli doesn't even acknowledge Jacob's interjection, "But it must be refined. You must find what you think is worth something in you and dig deep, deep below the surface. You must blast yourself out of your comfort zone, which I think it is safe to say has already happened. You must go through trials. You must go through the painful refining process. It is also safe to say you have already experienced some of that. But if you keep looking you will be purified and you will be like pure gold refined in the fire. You will shine Jacob! We have risked all and invested everything in you. We believe in you. Let us help you through to the other side. Stop fighting this."

Jacob continues to resist, "What exactly are you talking about? I'm just a man, a broken man at that. Maybe you should look somewhere else for a better candidate? I'm sure there must be better men than me. Look around there are billions of people in the world. I'm sure many of them are better than I am."

Eli interrupts him, "You are the one we want. There is a battle raging right now. And it is for YOU! You must be strong. You have to be strong. No matter what may come your way. Don't listen to the screams or the tumults. Don't look in the storm or in the fire. Quietly listen to the still small voice in you that guides you home and you will make it. We are here for you. We will help you."

Eli walks out. Jacob looks to have peace for the first time in a long time. He calls after Eli as he leaves. With tears of hope and humility he says, "I will make it through, Eli. Wisdom is priceless. And you're right, it's not found in the land of the living, but I have found it. It's nice to finally have some hope.

I swear to you if I ever make it out of this, if I ever do find peace I will never be the same. I will appreciate every breath! I will drink life in! I will be an encouragement! I will help those in need! I will have compassion! I will be there! I will make it out! I will! The greatest treasure is to have a second chance and use it wisely. And I will. I will use my second chance wisely.

Whoever hears me will speak well of me, and those who see me will commend me, because I will rescue the poor who cry for help, and the fatherless who have no one to assist them. I will help the dying man and I will make the widow's heart sing. I will be eyes to the blind and feet to the lame. I will be a father to the needy. I will take up the case of the stranger. I will break the fangs of the wicked and snatch the victims from their mouth.

I thought I was untouchable. I thought I would die of old age in my own house, but I was wrong. I thought I would never fall, but I was wrong. I am but a man.

I am fragile and weak and lost. I need help, but in return I will gladly repay you for the rest of my days. I will change my ways. I will lose my pride. I am sorry. Please guide me to the way home. Please! I am ready!"

Back in the courtroom the camera pulls away and the courtroom has once again been watching Jacob. Joseph is beaming that Jacob is finally doing the right thing. Tears of joy are streaming down his face. He gains his composure. Lucy is holding her ears and seems to be in pain.

Joseph looks at the judge, "He has been tested and he still stands true! I knew it! I knew it! How rare it is to find a good man, but we have done it! He has stood in the face of adversity and resisted the temptation to fall even though he had every reason to."

Lucy is disgusted, "So what! He's a good man. Big deal. He still has to find his way out and until then he is still mine to torment. He will have to get past me to escape and I don't see that happening. Do you want to just make a plea deal now… or are you going to keep this charade going?"

Joseph stands a little taller, "I'll see it through to the end. He is worth it. Your honor, I request a quickening of Jacob's spirit and a guide for my client."

Lucy cringes and speaks up quickly, "I object. One word of hope can't bring all this. You are stacking the odds against me. This is unfair."

The judge calmly says, "Overruled. It will be as you ask, Joseph. Send a guide. Send Eli back."

Joseph perks up, "Your honor...I would like to request that… I… could be Jacob's guide. My true image."
The judge pauses, "Granted."

Chapter 7 – This is How it Ends

Joseph walks into Jacob's room. He is wearing a suit and is dressed like a lawyer. Jacob looks at Joseph and he seems to know him. There is something familiar about his mannerisms, his cadence, and his spirit that Jacob identifies with. He tilts his head to the side and smiles, "Do I.... know ....you?"

Joseph smiles back at him, "I believe you do. Let me introduce myself. My name is Joseph and I am your attorney."

Jacob is confused, "Attorney? My attorney's name is Ed?"

Joseph ignores his confusion, "Yes, I am your defense and I am your council. I am the one who has protected and guided you to this point."

Jacob is very confused, "Guided me to what point exactly? You look familiar, but I don't believe we have met. Am I wrong?"

Joseph continues, "Do you ever feel like your entire life has been preparation for one thing? Like every thing has been woven together for a higher purpose?"

Jacob ponders for a moment, "Maybe? I suppose? Explain?"

Joseph puts his hand on Jacob's shoulder, "Now I will show you what you can not see. There are no secrets, Jacob. We have seen everything you have ever done. Every thought, every word, every thing. We know your motivations and your fears. We know what you say and do when no one else is around. We have seen everything."

Jacob falls to his knees and bows his head in shame.

Jacob whispers quietly, "So this is my judgment day?" He pauses, "All I ever wanted to do was be proud of myself when I finally had to give an account for my life. But I have failed. I'm so ashamed. I'm so sorry. I'm so sorry." He starts crying. He is beyond broken by this point. All the pain that has been bottled up inside of him finds its way out in a sad weeping.

Joseph grabs Jacob's hands and lifts him, "Rise to your feet Jacob Mason and let me finish. We have seen your deeds ...and we have found no fault in you. You are a good man with a pure heart, which is a rare thing. You have been tested and you have stood true. Even though the world raged against you, you held strong. We are proud...I am proud of you. I couldn't have asked for better than you."

Jacob is shocked, "I'm not good. How can you know all my deeds and say that I am a good man?" He is still crying, "I was tempted to do so many things."

Joseph reassures him, "There is a difference between being tempted to do something and actually doing it. The amazing thing is that you didn't do any of the things you were tempted to do. Believe me, I know how strong the temptation was. Lucy is good at what she does."

Jacob thinks for a moment, "Who in the world is Lucy?"

Joseph explains, "She is your accuser, your prosecutor and your temptress. She is the one that wants to sift you through her fingers like sand. She is your enemy that would love nothing more than to see you die. She is the one that struggles to keep you locked inside your mind when life is right there knocking at your door."

Jacob is upset, "Why would anyone want to do that?"

Joseph continues, "I have to go back a little farther to explain that."

Jacob is eagerly listening. He is confused by everything, but somehow it makes sense to him and feels strangely familiar, "Please do. I want to hear more."

Joseph goes on, "You see I was in a coma at one time too. I was an only child and my mother had died. My father loved me dearly and spent all his time with me until I came out. After I came out my father and I created the Born Again program to help others in the same condition. All I wanted to do was help people out because I know what a living hell it can be in here. We had a helper named Lucy. She and I would go into the minds of the patients and talk them out. We would help them. We were like the angels in their mind that led them to the door back to life with their families and friends.

At some point Lucy started to figure out that there is a lot of power when the world you live in has no limits. She began to experiment and found that she could do anything she wanted. She started liking the power and it became like an addiction for her. We noticed a change in her, but we were busy and thought she was just a little frazzled from all the extra work.

She came in the hospital late one night and reprogrammed the mainframe. She locked herself deep inside the computer and has enjoyed the power of tormenting these poor lost souls ever since. Souls like you."

Jacob is taken aback, "Why don't you just get her out?"

Joseph shakes his head, "That is the tricky part. The only way to get her out is to turn off the mainframe and restart the computer."

Jacob huffs, "So, what's the problem. Do it."

Joseph explains, "The problem is that to do that we have to turn off all the power in the hospital. If we do that than everyone that is on life support will die. Life is a precious thing and I can't justify taking innocent lives to potentially save someone else's life. We just have to work around her until they are all out or until she has a change of heart, which at this point seems highly unlikely."

Jacob replies, "That is terrible! How do you deal with that? She has made a difficult job almost impossible."

Joseph nods and shrugs, "So now it comes back to you. Now that you know the truth what do you choose to do with it?"

Jacob is almost defensive, "What am I supposed to do? I don't know what to do. I am lost!"

Joseph smiles, "That is the first step. Admitting that you are lost and that you need help."

Jacob perks up, "Well, that wasn't too hard. What's the second step?"

Joseph puts his hand out, "Will you follow me? I know the way that leads to life. It isn't easy. You can't look to the left or to the right, no matter what happens. You must keep focused. You must know that even if death seems imminent that it isn't real."

Jacob hesitates, "Am I going to have to die?"

Joseph smiles, "Die to this world? Yes. But when you do die to this world, you open your eyes to the next where your real life awaits you."

Jacob contemplates his own death and what that might feel like. He imagines all the ways he might be asked to die. He cringes. He thinks of his life here before the accident and the scandals. He thinks about all he will leave behind. What if he isn't rich in the real world? What if he has no status? What if he is just some schmuck in a world full of schmucks? What if he has to relearn and unlearn everything he knows to be true? All these thoughts race through his mind.

"Is there an easier way? How about if I just pay you or something. I can afford any price and then you can just do the work since you know the way and I don't."

Joseph is offended, "What are you going to give me that is worth anything? Everything you own is just a thought! It's just your imagination. What good does that do any of us? You are the treasure, Jacob. You are what we fight for! And if you don't do your part, then the whole thing is in vain.

Do you know how much effort and money and time and equipment has been put into bringing you back to life?"

Jacob hangs his head, "How could I?"

Joseph raises his voice, "The lives of many good people and a fortune that you couldn't fathom! It took years and years of work and a lifetime of dedication and discipline and patience just so that you can stand at this moment of decision. Others never had this opportunity, but you have it. Because of all they have sacrificed you have been given this precious chance. Don't waste this. Don't treat it as trivial. You see it goes a little deeper than I let on."

Jacob feels scolded, "How much deeper could it possibly go?"

Joseph looks at Jacob very seriously and says, "You are the last one."

Jacob is confused, "The last what?"

Joseph pauses, "Remember when I said that when all the people wake up that we can get Lucy out." Jacob nods. "You are the last one. She doesn't know it. We have put in virtual people to keep her busy. We have kept you busy. But Jacob, you are it! You either make it through and wake up or ...."

Jacob panics, "Or what?"

Joseph looks down, "Or... you die! There isn't much time. The key that you have been looking for is inside of you. Will you follow me?"

Jacob gets serious, "Yes, of course. Where are we going?"

Joseph seems to go in a different direction, "It is harder for a rich man to come to life than for a camel to go through the eye of a needle."

Jacob retorts, "Then it is impossible! How can a camel go through that tiny hole in a sewing needle?"

Joseph goes on, "Not a sewing needle. Many people don't now this but in ancient times, cities had walls around them to protect them from enemies. They had huge gates that were shut at night, but if you had trouble and had to come in late then what?

Jacob replies, "Tough! Wait until morning, I guess?"

Joseph continues, "Incorrect, then there was the eye of the needle. It was a small door that a man could go through, but wasn't big enough for intruders to do much damage through."

Jacob is intrigued, "I was unaware of that. It's pretty smart really."

Joseph keeps going, "For a camel to go through the eye of the needle, it would have to do three things.

1) Take everything off it's back.
2) Get down on its knees.
3) Obey its master even though it couldn't see where it was going."

Jacob looks up, "I never knew that. I always thought it was a sewing needle. Interesting."

Joseph goes on "A rich man is self-righteous, prideful, and depends on no one but himself. He is arrogant and feels he is better than others around him. For a rich man to lose everything he has is hard for him. For a rich man to humble himself and get on his knees is difficult for his pride. For him to obey is not in his nature. People should listen to him or so he thinks. For a rich man to ask for help isn't easy for him. For a rich man to put someone else's life before his own is rare. It is easier for a camel to go through the eye of a needle. Now, do you see?"

Jacob laughs, "I am the rich man you are talking about, aren't I? I have lost everything anyway. And I know I need help. I am a humble man. Please help me. I will follow."

Joseph looks at him and says, "Then follow me."

Joseph walks out of the room and disappears. Jacob chases him, but finds nothing. He runs outside and there is a terrible storm. The wind is very strong. The rain is beating down heavily. He sees a priest across the street. He knows that Joseph takes on the image of other people so he runs over to him. The rain is cold and stings. The wind is blowing so hard he can barely see.

Jacob says to the priest, "Did you see a man in a suit just a second ago? He is my lawyer."

The priest shakes his head, "No one has come out here except you. There is no one here but you. You are alone. It is just you and me here Jacob." The priest smiles wickedly. "This whole life you think you have been living has been nothing more than a test for as far back as you can remember. Nothing that you think is real is actually real at all. Do you even know why you are here?"

Jacob is confused, but wants answers, "Tell me."

The priest scowls, "You are being tested. You are being tried. And you have been found wanting. You fail. Why couldn't you just keep up? Do you hear me? You fail! What have you done?"

Jacob looks discouraged and starts to lose heart. Then he remembers the words of the lion saying, "Things aren't always what they appear. Don't you think it's time to move on?"

Jacob lifts his head, "Aren't you supposed to be a man of God? Have some hope. I haven't failed yet. You should reconsider which side you are on." Jacob perks up and runs down the alley away from the priest.

The priest calls after him, "Don't bother trying. You have failed already! Do you hear me? You are nothing but a failure!" As Jacob runs away the priest keeps hurling insults at him.

Jacob runs to the end of the alley and sees Bill standing outside in the rain. Bill calls out to him, "Jacob, stop! It's me Bill. I told you about my friend Jezebel, the prophetess, didn't I? She can help you to find your way. She can see things that we can't see. She has a direct line to God himself. Come inside for a while and we'll help you."

Jacob steps in out of the rain to an abandoned building. There is a fire burning in a trashcan in the middle of the room. Jezebel closes her eyes and puts her hand on Jacob's forehead. Her eyes roll back in her head. She convulses. Her eyes twitch back and forth.

With one hand on his forehead and the other hand raised to the sky she says loudly, "I see inside your mind. I see inside your soul, into the blackness, into the secret places. Into the muck and mire that consumes you! You are going full speed ahead in the wrong direction. You should go that way!"

She points back to the priest, who has walked up closer to him.

She continues, "You should spend some time trying to seek some help. Maybe see a psychiatrist? I have a friend that would be great for you. Therapy will fix everything. It can be as it was. Liars have led you astray. Come with us and it will all be OK."

Jacob resists the lies, "No. This isn't real. I know it isn't! I must find Joseph! You only want to deceive me and keep me here. I won't stay! Do you hear me! I am going home! I am going home and I'm not afraid! Put that in your crystal ball and smoke it."

Crystal shows up out of nowhere and says, "Funny that my name should come up in all this, don't you think? Why did you have to let it come to this? All I wanted to do was be your friend and lover. Is that so wrong? Is it? I just want some company from a good man. It's not too late. I will give you one more chance to join me and then I will get nasty. What's it going to be?"

Jacob's strength is growing, "Never! You can't distract me. I am focused. I have been quickened. And I am going to be with my real family. I am on my way home! I am going to live again!"

Crystal laughs at him, "Let's talk about your real family for a minute. Where are they now? They don't care about you. They aren't even real. You have no family! We are your family. We are here for you, not them! Let them show themselves. I'll wait."

Jacob is distraught, "Be quiet! They love me. Just because I can't see them doesn't mean they aren't there. That's what faith is isn't it, knowing something and believing in the truth even though you can't see it and even though the world around you screams otherwise. I believe! I have faith! I know where I am going! I know that my redeemer lives and I know his name! I am tired of being weak. I am going home!"

Lucy walks up and the flames in the trashcan consume the entire building. Snake has Jacob's children hostage with a knife to Rose's throat. Lucy puffs up temporarily and then gets quiet, "Why did it have to come to this? I told you it would get nasty if you didn't yield." She looks at Snake, "Kill his children!"

Jacob cries out, "No! Wait! Anything but that!"

Lucy smiles a wicked grin, "A weakness? Perfect. We found the crack."

Jacob begs, "Please don't hurt them. I'm sorry."

Jacob falls to his knees

"I don't care if this is real. I love my children. I can't stand by and watch them die. Not again."

Lucy comes close to Jacob, "So you'll bow to me, then?"

Jacob looks defeated, "I…I can't."

Lucy snaps back, "Well, we have a dilemma then, don't we? You won't bow, but if you don't bow then I will have Snake slice your children into tiny pieces... slowly, while you are forced to watch. You will hear the echoes of their cries for all eternity. And you will know that you could have stopped it, but were too stubborn and too stupid to make a simple gesture to me."

Jacob drops his head. He gets quiet. A tear comes to his eye, "Please, don't!"

Jacob pauses and looks like he is going to give up when he looks in the distance. The lion is all tied up.

The lion roars, "Why have you held back your courage? Why do you still want to run? You must turn and face your fears. You are better than them. No regrets, Jacob. No regrets. Stand strong! I am with you! Be brave!"

Jacob thinks for a moment and then yells at Lucy, "Wait!" She turns around. "Take me instead. Kill me instead. Surely, that will give you some sick pleasure and then you will win. Just don't hurt them. It isn't right. Please, take me instead."

Lucy laughs loudly, "I thought you would never ask. Very well. Let the brats go." The children disappear. "Take Jacob instead. Normally, I would torture you for a while, but I'm afraid you might change your mind and beg for mercy."

Jacob is obstinate, "I won't beg for anything from you. I would rather die. Make it quick. I'm ready."

Snake throws the knife into Jacob's chest and he falls to the ground. He is still grasping for breath. Lucy walks up and steps on his throat.

She gloats, "If I can't have you then you must die. It sucks to be you, doesn't it? Well, that sure was a righteous thing you just did. The problem is that when you die in here... you really die out there too. You fool! And you actually chose it for yourself, too. Pathetic!"

Lucy stomps the knife farther into Jacob's chest. He struggles for air and he breathes his last. He collapses. Lucy squeals with glee, "Oh how I love spilling the blood of the righteous."

Jacob dies. He dies in front of Lucy but also in the hospital, the real one. All Jacob's family stands around his bed. There are no sores on him. He looks like a sleeping angel. The family is crying. They have lost all hope.

Jacob is dead. The monitor next to his bed is flat lining. The doctors are putting away paddles from trying to shock him back to life. Joseph is in the virtual reality booth with tears streaming down his cheeks. There is a strange silence.

Chapter 8 – The After Life

Jacob lies lifeless in the dark, but then the sun starts to rise. Jacob wakes up in the clouds. There is a line of people as far as the eye can see. All his friends and family, acquaintances, workers, business associates, the nurses, hospital workers, everyone he has ever known. They each come to him one by one and thank him for being such a good man.

The nurse Michael says, "You are a good man Jacob. These people are here to pay their respects to a truly good man... YOU are that man. We are proud of you. You gave your life willingly in exchange for others, without promise of reward and with the knowledge that you would not have your own life back. No greater love is there than this. Your darkness will be as the noonday sun. You have arrived!

Jacob is so confused. He can't even speak. Eli walks up to him, "Thank you, Jacob. Thank you for listening to me. Not many do. I am proud of you."

A nurse walks up, "You stood strong to the end, Jacob. I have rarely seen a man go through as much as you have gone through. But to do all that and then come out shining is almost unheard of. I am proud to know you."

Jacob's lawyer Ed is next, "Thank you, Jacob. You gave a young ambitious man a job when no one else would. You changed my life. You were always a good friend. I always looked up to you. You gave me courage when life wasn't on my side. I am proud to know you."

His friend Frank walks up cautiously, "Thank you, Jacob for always being my friend. You know I didn't really have an affair with your wife, don't you? That was just in your head. We're still friends, right?" Frank flinches and backs off. Jacob is cautious, but hugs Frank. He is happy to have his friend back.

His secretary Nancy walks up, "I couldn't have asked for a better boss. I always held my head a little higher when I was asked where I worked. It was an honor to work for you."

His wife Laura peeks around the people in front of her. She runs up and hugs him, "What a wonderful man you are! A wife couldn't ask for a better man to be married to. You are all I ever wanted. I am proud to be Mrs. Jacob Mason! I love you!" She kisses him over and over.

Jacob hears his son Taylor. He looks and then leans down on one knee. Taylor runs up and hugs Jacob's neck. Jacob is in tears. "I love you Daddy. I love you Daddy!"

He hears his daughter. She runs up and hugs him as well, "I love you Daddy. I love you Daddy. I love you Daddy."

With his whole family hugging him the lion walks up, "I guess you found me after all, didn't you? You didn't run in the face of danger. You didn't cower under evil's sway. You deserve everything that is coming to you. It couldn't have happened to a better guy. I am proud to know you.
You stood the test. You are beautiful. You are worthy. There is nothing to be ashamed of. We are all proud of you. But I hate for you to die. Don't you think it's time to be born again?"

Jacob is confused, "Isn't that what this is?"

Joseph walks up to him, "No, you are dead on the table. What you see and hear is the voices of the ones that love you, the ones that will mourn your loss if you leave us. This is my last chance to get you back. You have people that love you, people that believe in you, people that look up to you. They haven't left your side since the plague."

Jacob is so confused, "What plague?"

Joseph shakes his head, "Do you still not remember? A third of the population fell to a terrible plague that was dropped on us by an enemy named Lucy. We have captured her now. Thanks, in part, to you of course. But we don't want to lose you. Wake up Jacob. Come with me."

Jacob is in a state of emotional overload, "People love me? People really love me?"

Joseph snickers, "Of course! Did you ever doubt? Why would we go to all this trouble if we didn't love you?"

Joseph takes Jacob's hand and they walk across a beautiful lake with a white wall at the far end of it. Everything is very bright. The wall is full of jewels and has a gate that is made of a pearl. Beyond the gate is a city made of pure gold. Joseph smiles, "Come on, let's get you home."

Jacob stops, "What about you?"

Joseph has sadness in his eyes, "Where I am going, you cannot go yet. In this city, in your eternal home, there is no more pain. There is no more sorrow. There is no more death. There are no more tears. There is no night there. Now you see in part and you know in part, but in a moment you will know fully and you will see with your own eyes. Justice is there if you wait long enough for it."

Jacob smiles, "Yes, I suppose you are right."

Joseph reassures Jacob, "By your own words you have been saved. This is where I have to leave you. Go home, Jacob."

Jacob is sad, "But what about you? Aren't you coming?"

Joseph looks weak, "I can't. I paid the price for you. I gave my life for yours. Don't make it a waste. I wouldn't have done it for just anyone. It has been an honor knowing you, Jacob. While you laid on the table bleeding I gave my blood for you so you could live. They are doing the transfusion now. I will see you again. I will be with you always. Always watching. Always helping. I am your lawyer. I am your defense and your council. I love you. You gave your life for another and now I am giving my life for you.

Go. You can't stay on this side for too long. You have people that love you. I'll see you again in our eternal home. Perhaps they will find a way to bring me back, but if not at least I died for a worthy cause. At least I died for a righteous man. It was an honor. Open the door, Jacob. It is time."

He throws Jacob a key.

Jacob starts sobbing. He sees the gravity of the situation, "No, you must come too! Wake up with me. We will find a way."

Jacob hugs Joseph and refuses to let go. Joseph pushes him through the door and Jacob cries out, "I will never forget you! I will find a way to repay you!"

Joseph whispers, "You already have. I'll see you on the other side."

Jacob's eyes open. He is in the hospital. His family is there hugging him. They are so excited. They are calling other family members back in the room. "He is alive!" They are shouting. "He was dead, but now he is alive!"

Joseph is still hooked up to the virtual reality machine. He looks completely drained. He is turning grey because he is now dead. Even though he is the true hero in this story he goes mostly unnoticed. Then Jacob looks over and sees his body lying there. He whispers, "I will never forget you! I will find a way to repay you. Thank you. Thank you for everything. Thank you for my life."

I never knew a man like Jacob until then. He gave me hope in a fallen world. As for Jacob, His wife never cheated on him, his children grew up to be strong, his reputation was esteemed among all those who knew him, and his merger with Hope Technologies went through without a problem. In the end Jacob was twice as rich as he was before.

He didn't just save his wallet, though. You see Jacob had found the treasure that is priceless. The treasure that is in us all, if we will hold fast to what is right no matter the cost. He took his second chance at life and ran with it. He drank life in. He was an encouragement to all those around him! He helped those in need! He had compassion! He made it out! The greatest treasure is not the size of your bank account, but to have a second chance and use it wisely. And he did just that.

Whoever knew him spoke well of him, and those who saw him commended him, because he rescued the poor who cried for help, and the fatherless who had no one to assist them. He helped the dying man and made the widow's heart sing. He was eyes to the blind and feet to the lame. He was a father to the needy. He took up the case of the stranger. He broke the fangs of the wicked and snatched the victims from their mouth.

He was untouchable. He died of old age in his own house. He never fell. He made a promise to me that in return for his life he would gladly repay his debt to me for the rest of his days. "I will change my ways", he said. "I will lose my pride. I am sorry. Please guide me to the way home. Please!" He kept his promise, like I knew he would. The latter part of Jacob's life was more prosperous than the first part. He lived a long and wonderful life and was an inspiration to all those who knew him, ...including me.

And just like the gold that is refined in the fire, Jacob was the treasure that was left after the storm. He dug deep. He paid the price. He was blasted from his comfort zone. He was broken down and tried, but in the end only what was pure was left. Jacob was not alone...and neither are you. Shine in the darkness. Rise to the top. Don't give up! You are not alone! You are never alone! The road is deeply personal and unique, but it is yours and I want you to be proud when you have to give an account for your life as well. Don't run from your courage!

The End

Made in the USA
Middletown, DE
17 April 2018